With extra sparkly thanks to Jo Podmore

Emma Thomson's
felicity Wishes®

FELICITY WISHES: FASHION MAGIC
by Emma Thomson

British Library Cataloguing in Publication Data
A catalogue record of this book is available from the British Library.
ISBN 0-340-88183-6
Felicity Wishes © 2000 Emma Thomson.
Licensed by White Lion Publishing.
Felicity Wishes: Fashion Magic © 2004 Emma Thomson.

The right of Emma Thomson to be identified as the author
and illustrator of this Work has been asserted by WLP
in accordance with the Copyright, Designs and Patents Act 1988.

First HB edition published 2004
10 9 8 7 6 5 4 3 2 1

Published by Hodder Children's Books, a division of Hodder Headline Limited,
338 Euston Road, London, NW1 3BH

Printed in China

Emma Thomson's

felicity Wishes®

Fashion Magic

Hodder
Children's
Books

A division of Hodder Headline Limited

Felicity Wishes and her friends were walking into Little Blossoming, gossiping about everything and nothing.

Suddenly, Polly squealed with delight. "Look at this!" she cried pointing to a poster. "I've always wanted to be a model fairy!"

Felicity looked dreamily up at the sky. I can just see myself on a catwalk in a sparkly dress the colour of candyfloss, she thought.

"Let's do it!" said Holly as she began to walk down the High Street with her hands on her hips, practising her catwalk moves.

"But what will we wear?" asked Daisy.

STAR ST
FAIRY FASHION SHOW
MODEL FAIRIES WANTED
wiggle! wiggle!

Felicity and Polly headed straight to Fairy Belle Boutique on the corner of the High Street.

There were lots of twinkly outfits on display. "I'm terrible at choosing clothes," said Polly glumly. "I can never decide what looks good on me."

"It's easy when you know how," said Felicity. "All you need to do is choose an outfit that suits your personality and feels good."

Polly emerged from the changing room in a very dainty dress. "That looks perfect on you Pol," gasped Felicity.

Fairy Fashion Card

Favourite colour ....

Shoe size ....

Height ....

Eye colour ....

Hair colour ....

Ideal style ....

The next day, Felicity had just sat down to think about what she was going to wear to the Fashion Show when the doorbell rang.

Holly stood on the doorstep looking very flustered. "I can't find anything to wear to the Fashion Show! Do you have something I could borrow?" she said hopefully.

"Come upstairs!" said Felicity, leading the way. "Most of my dresses are pink, but I have some wonderful accessories that can transform the look of any outfit."

Holly's crown nearly pinged off with delight.

FAIRY TIPS FOR ACCESSORIES

❋ Buy a bagful of string and beads to design your own inexpensive accessories.

❋ Feather boas and pieces of shiny fabric look great around your shoulders.

❋ Don't be afraid to pair your everyday clothes with a sparkly, party-time hair accessory.

❋ Wear fun bracelets and a sparkly bag to look individual.

Ribbons & Bows

After an exhausting morning, Felicity decided to visit The Wednesday Market. She was bound to find a new outfit there.

Felicity was quite literally up to her nose in ribbons and bows when Daisy came flying over.

"I need your help Felicity," pleaded Daisy. "I want to transform an old dress for the Fashion Show but I don't know where to start."

"Look no further!" said Felicity. "There's lots of lovely things here we can sew onto your dress to give it a magical make-over."

TOP TIPS TO TRANSFORM ANY OUTFIT

Throw a clothes swapping party with your friends and exchange clothes you've grown tired of.

Visit second-hand shops or charity shops for great buys.

Reinvent last year's clothes by adding beads, buttons and ribbons.

Borrow clothes from a friend's wardrobe for a new look.

When Felicity got home that evening she slumped on her bed. She had never sewn so many flowers onto one dress before, but it was worth it. Daisy simply sparkled in her new outfit.

"What am I going to wear?" Felicity despaired. "Everyone has a beautiful outfit to wear except me."

Felicity began to try on every item of clothing she owned. "There must be something here that will look good," she said determinedly.

But all Felicity found was what not to wear!

What not to wear

1. Colours that clash.
2. Clothes that are two sizes too small.
3. Dresses that look like tents!
4. Shoes that hurt your feet.
5. Checks with spots or stripes.

As Felicity sat
on her bedroom floor,
in a mountain of mess,
there was a sudden tap at the window.

"Oh Polly," said an exhausted Felicity. "I've got clothes everywhere and can't find anything to wear for the Fashion Show tomorrow."

"Felicity, you are so disorganised," despaired Polly. "Let's start by arranging your clothes into piles."

At the bottom of the messy pile, something caught Felicity's eye. "My favourite pink dress!" said Felicity, waving a dry-cleaning ticket. "I had forgotten all about it – it will be perfect for the Fashion Show."

POLLY'S
TIDY WARDROBE TIPS

Take any clothes that no longer fit or you have never worn to the charity shop.

Throw away any coat hangers which are no longer of use.

Clear out all the shoes you refuse to wear.

Fold all your clothes neatly to make more space.

Separate your clothes into winter, summer, casual and party outfits.

Help keep your clothes fresh by adding a bag of lavender to your wardrobe.

Put all the clutter at the bottom of your wardrobe in a box.

Finally, it was the day of the Fashion Show. There was lots of nervous giggling and excitement backstage amongst the fairies taking part, especially Felicity, Holly, Polly and Daisy.

Each glittering fairy waited patiently for their turn to wow the audience.

When the time came, Felicity and her friends glided stylishly down the catwalk to great applause.

If only magical days like this could last forever, thought Felicity as she held her head up high and smiled at the audience.

Flying around frantically after the show,
Felicity finally found her three fairy friends
swapping stories about their dazzling day.

"Guess what?" she puffed. "'The Daily Flutter'
want to do an article on our outfits. They want
all our top fashion tips and have promised to put
our photos on the front cover!"

"Wow! That's fantastic news," chorused the fairies.

"This is our chance," said Felicity excitedly to
her friends, "to spread a bit of fashion magic
everywhere!"

The Daily Flutter

FREE

WEATHER TODAY: SUNNY

TUESDAY'S EDITION

FASHION SHOW FAIRIES

Get dressed before putting on your make-up.

You don't have to spend a fortune on buying clothes; second-hand shops have great buys.

Don't be afraid to experiment with different mix and match schemes.

Go colour crazy and try out different colour combinations.

Tear out ideas from fashion magazines and catalogues.

Style really comes from having confidence in yourself.

With this fashion
book comes a dazzling
Felicity wish:

Open this book with your eyes closed
and let it fall open on any page.
Think of a wish you always dreamed
would come true and whisper it into
the page three times.

Keep this book in a safe place and,
maybe, one day, your wish
might just come true.

Love felicity
x